The Mystery of the Blue Ring

"Maybe you left the ring at home," Sherri said.

Emily shook her head. "I wore it to school yesterday. I had it in art."

"She's right," said Dawn. "I saw it on the art room sink."

Sherri's eyes opened wide. "Maybe you took it, Dawn."

Beast turned around. "You took Emily's unicorn last time."

Dawn looked at the other kids.

All of them were looking at her.

"I didn't take the ring," she whispered.

Nobody said anything. Maybe nobody believed her.

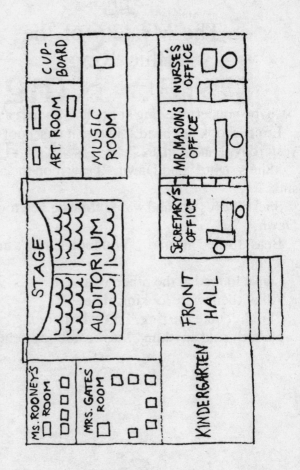

POLK ST. SCHOOL

The Mystery of the Blue Ring

PATRICIA REILLY GIFF

Illustrated by Blanche Sims

YOUNG
LIONS

First published in the USA 1987 by Dell Publishing
First published in Great Britain 1989 by Young Lions

Young Lions is an imprint of
the Children's Division, part of
the Collins Publishing Group
8 Grafton Street, London W1X 3LA

Text copyright © 1987 by Patricia Reilly Giff
Illustrations copyright © 1987 by Blanche Sims
All rights reserved

Printed in Great Britain
by William Collins Sons & Co. Ltd, Glasgow

For my dear Catherine Van Slyck
with love

Chapter 1

It was Thursday afternoon.

Dawn Bosco turned the page of her book. She wanted to get to the end before art.

She had to find out about the secret in the old house.

Ms Rooney looked up. "Dawn, are you listening?"

Dawn closed her book.

"Today is Good Vegetable Day," said Ms Rooney.

Dawn rolled her pencil down her desk.

She hated vegetables.

She thought about the girl in her book, Diane the Detective.

Dawn wished she could be a detective, too.

She wished she could solve a mystery. A scary one.

"Who has a favourite vegetable?" asked Ms Rooney.

Jason Bazyk waved his hand. "Apples," he said.

"That's not a vegetable," said Timothy Barbiero.

"How about spinach?" asked Ms Rooney. "Or cabbage?"

"Yuck," Dawn said.

Next to her, Emily Arrow said yuck, too.

Dawn looked at Emily.

Sometimes they were friends. Sometimes they weren't.

She had done something bad to Emily.

She had taken her unicorn.

That was weeks ago, though. She had given it back.

Maybe Emily didn't remember it any more. Dawn hoped not.

The bell rang. It was time for art.

Dawn raced to the front of the line. She edged in ahead of Emily.

Dawn loved to be first.

Emily gave her a little push.

Emily liked to be first, too.

They marched into the art room.

On every table were lumps of grey stuff. There were little bowls of water, too.

Dawn wondered what they were for.

Mrs Kara, the art teacher, clapped her hands. "Today is Good Vegetable Day."

"I'm sick of vegetables," said Jason.

Dawn was sick of vegetables, too. She

poked her finger into the grey stuff.

It was soft. Gooey.

It felt like chewing gum.

Mrs Kara held up a piece. "This is clay," she said.

Dawn wrinkled her nose. At home her clay was red and yellow and green. Not yucky grey.

"We are going to make Good Vegetables," said Mrs Kara. "Watch. I'm going to make a head of lettuce."

Mrs Kara rolled a fat ball. She made a curly top.

She kept wetting her lettuce with her fingers. "The water makes it easier to shape," she said.

Dawn looked out of the window. If only she could find a mystery!

Mrs Kara held up her grey lettuce.

Jill Simon started to cry. "I don't know how to do it."

"Of course you do," said Mrs Kara. "Now, everyone pick a vegetable."

Dawn pulled at her clay. She'd make a cucumber. That would be easy.

Emily Arrow put up her hand. "I'm going to make a cucumber."

"Me, too," said Dawn.

Mrs Kara frowned a little. "Make something else, Dawn."

Dawn crossed her eyes at Emily.

She tried to think of something else to make.

Beast was making a string bean. He mashed the clay against the table.

He was making a big mess.

Jill Simon was making an onion. It looked like a fat grey ball with lines.

Dawn dug into her own clay.

She made a fat carrot.

It was much better than Emily's cucumber.

Emily's cucumber was too fat at one end. It was too skinny at the other. It looked like a mouse.

"We'll put the vegetables on the windowsill," said Mrs Kara. "Everyone will see them."

Dawn rushed to finish first. Her hands were grey. So were her nails.

"Hurry," said Mrs Kara. "It's almost time to go home."

Dawn went to the art room cupboard to wash.

A minute later, Emily came in. So did Sherri Dent and Jill and Linda Lorca.

The water in the sink was icy cold.

They all put their hands in it.

Everyone was laughing.

Everyone but Dawn and Emily.

Emily was taking up too much room, Dawn thought.

She gave her a little push.

Emily pushed back.

A gold ring lay on the ledge of the sink.

Dawn poked it back against the wall. She didn't want it to go down the drain.

"Move over," she told Emily.

"You move over, carrot legs," Emily told her.

Dawn sniffed. "You don't know beans from grapes." She took a piece of brown paper to dry her hands.

She marched out of the cupboard.

She wished she could find a crime right now.

She'd solve it in two minutes.
Emily would be sorry.
Very sorry.

Chapter 2

The next morning, Dawn waited at the corner.

She stamped up and down in her new cowgirl boots.

Her grandmother had bought them for her.

Noni bought her everything. Almost everything.

"Hi," Dawn called to Carmen, the crossing guard.

Carmen didn't call back. She was too busy. She waved her arms around. Dawn waved her arms around, too.

She'd love to wear a blue hat and a badge.

She'd love to tell people what to do.

17

She'd tell the good kids to cross first.

She'd make the bad kids cross last.

She'd make Emily Arrow stand on the corner forever.

Carmen held up her hand.

A green car stopped. So did a white one.

Dawn held up her hand, too.

Nothing happened.

Carmen smiled at her. "You can cross now."

Dawn started across the street.

"What's cooking, Cookie?" Carmen asked.

Carmen said that every day.

Dawn lifted one foot high in the air.

"New tights?" Carmen asked.

Dawn shook her head. Her tights were a hundred years old. They had a hole in the toe.

"Cowgirl boots," she said.

"Nice." Carmen held up her hand. "Have a good Friday."

Dawn marched into the Polk Street School. She went down the hall into Room 113.

She hoped everyone could see her boots.

She made believe they had a speck on them.

She bent down to clean them off.

Jason bumped into her. He nearly knocked her over.

"Sorry," he yelled. He slid out of her way.

"Not so loud, Jason," said Ms Rooney.

Dawn shook her head. Jason was loud. He was loud even when he whispered.

Dawn sat in her seat, next to Emily Arrow.

Emily was running her unicorn across the desk. She was making snorting noises.

Dawn made herself say hello to Emily.

Her father said to be friends with everyone.

Emily didn't say hello back.

She snorted through her nose again.

Dawn wanted to smack her.

Then she saw that Emily was crying.

"What's the matter?" she asked.

Emily didn't answer.

At the front, Ms Rooney clapped her hands. "Settle down, everyone."

Beast slid into his seat. So did Jason and the rest of the class.

Dawn sat up straight.

"I have some serious news," Ms

Rooney said.

Ms Rooney looked angry.

No. Ms Rooney looked sad.

Dawn wondered why.

She looked at Emily out of the corner of her eye. Emily was crying hard.

"Something has happened," Ms Rooney said. "We have a mystery in Room 113."

Dawn took a breath. Terrific.

"Something is missing," Ms Rooney said.

Dawn looked around.

Everything seemed the same to her.

The flagpole was at the front of the room. The plants were on the windowsill.

The picture of George Washington was hanging on the wall.

Next to her, Emily Arrow was crying

harder.

"Matthew's head is missing," Beast said.

Matthew started to laugh. "You never even had a head," he told Beast.

"This is not the time for fooling around," said Ms Rooney.

"Shh," Dawn said to help her out.

Ms Rooney frowned a little. "Emily Arrow's ring is missing."

Dawn looked at Emily. Emily's eyes were red. So was her nose.

Dawn thought of her book, *The Secret of the Old House*.

A ring was even better than an old house.

She was sorry Emily's ring was gone.

She was glad, too.

She couldn't wait to solve the mystery.

Chapter 3

"It was my birthday ring," said Emily.

"The one with the blue stone?" Jason asked.

Emily nodded.

"The one with the crack in it?" Alex Walker asked.

"It was only a little crack," Emily said. "You couldn't even see it."

"I could," said Alex.

Dawn thought for a minute.

She knew she had seen that ring.

Where was it?

She closed her eyes.

Then she remembered. Yesterday afternoon.

It was on the art room sink. It was

full of soap.

Dawn put up her hand.

Ms Rooney looked at her.

"May I get a drink of water?" Dawn asked.

"Do it quickly," said Ms Rooney.

Dawn started out of the door.

Ms Rooney was saying, "Think hard, everyone. Did anyone see . . ."

Dawn took a quick drink of water.

She didn't really want water.

She wanted to go to the art room.

She'd get Emily's ring. She'd bring it to the classroom.

Emily would be thrilled.

Jason would say, "Dawn's a great detective."

Maybe Ms Rooney would excuse her from homework.

She hurried down the corridor.

Her cowgirl boots made clicking noises.

She clicked a little harder.

"Hey," said the monitor.

Dawn wanted to say "hey" back to him. He had a tough face, though.

She stopped clicking. She turned the corner.

Mrs Kara was in the art room.

Dawn put her head in. "I think Emily left something here."

Mrs Kara looked up. She had a spot of paint on her nose. "All right."

Dawn went into the cupboard. She took a deep breath.

She loved the smell in there.

She wished her father had the same floor-washing stuff.

She looked on the sink.

Just a piece of brown soap.

26

She picked up the mop.

Not there either.

Too bad.

Mrs Kara let her try in the art room.

She looked everywhere.

The ring was gone.

She sighed.

Dawn went down the corridor.

Jason was getting a drink. His cheeks were fat with water. He made crazy eyes at her.

Dawn laughed. She went into the classroom.

Ms Rooney was taking lunch money. There was a line at her desk.

Dawn stood behind Emily and Sherri.

Emily had stopped crying. She looked sad, though.

"Maybe you left the ring at home," Sherri said.

Emily shook her head.

"I bet you did," said Sherri.

"I wore it to school yesterday," Emily said. "I had it in art."

"She's right." Dawn leaned forward. "I saw it. It was on the art room sink."

Sherri's eyes opened wide. "Maybe you took it, Dawn."

"I did not."

"I bet you did," Sherri said.

"I even looked in the art room," Dawn said. "I tried to find it."

"Maybe it's in your pencil box," Sherri said to Dawn.

"Maybe," said Linda.

Dawn gave her milk money to Ms Rooney. "Chocolate," she said. "Please."

She took the pink ticket. Then she went back to her seat.

She pulled out her pencil box.

She took out her pencil with the tassel.

She took out her ruler.

She took out her rubber.

"See, smarty," she said to Sherri. "No ring."

Beast turned around. "You took Emily's unicorn last time."

Then Jill turned around, too. She looked as if she would cry.

Jill always looked that way.

Dawn looked at the other kids.

All of them were looking at her.

"I didn't take the ring," she whispered.

Nobody said anything.

Maybe nobody believed her.

Chapter 4

After school Dawn waited in the school playground.

She wanted to stay away from Sherri.

She didn't want to see the rest of the class, either.

Everyone thought she had taken Emily's ring.

Maybe even Jason Bazyk, the nicest boy she knew.

Dawn picked up a stick. She waved it in the air.

She made believe she was a cowgirl. She was rounding up cattle.

"Yip-pi-ai-ay," she said.

Then she broke the stick. She pushed it through the fence.

She didn't feel like playing cowgirl.

She didn't feel like playing anything.

She looked around. Everyone was gone.

She went out of the gate and started for the corner.

Carmen, the guard, was standing next to the letterbox.

All the cars were whizzing by.

"What's cooking, Cookie?" Carmen asked.

Dawn tried to smile.

Carmen pushed back her hat. "Lost all your get-up-and-go?"

"I suppose so," Dawn said.

"Tough cowgirl like you?"

Dawn raised one shoulder.

"Nobody liked your cowgirl boots?"

"I don't know," Dawn said.

Carmen put her whistle in her mouth.

She went to the middle of the street.

All the cars stopped.

"All right, Cookie," Carmen told her.

Dawn marched across the street.

The people in the cars were watching her.

She hoped they saw her cowgirl boots.

She almost forgot about Emily and the ring.

At the other side she stopped to wave at Carmen.

Carmen crossed the street after her.

Dawn hoped she wasn't going to ask what was the matter.

Dawn didn't want her to know about the ring.

Dawn didn't want her to think she had stolen it.

Carmen didn't ask, though.

She put her hand on Dawn's arm.

"Just chase that trouble away," she said.

"I will," Dawn said.

She went down the street. She wondered how you could chase trouble away.

Carmen called after her. "Get back your get-up-and-go."

"I will," Dawn said again. Carmen was right, she thought.

She put her head up.

She raised her boots high.

"Get up and go," she said in a loud voice.

A boy put his head over the fence. "Get up and gone," he said. He made a circle next to his ear with his finger. "Crazy."

Dawn pretended she hadn't seen him.

"Chase that trouble away," she said in her head.

She stopped at the corner.

How?

She felt a lump in her throat.

She swallowed.

There was only one way.

Find the ring.

Find the person who had taken it.

Yes.

"Get up and go," she said.

She raced down the street.

She had to get some stuff together.

Important stuff.

Detective stuff.

She went into the house.

She called hello to her father.

She said hi to Noni.

Noni was sewing a top for her. It had lace all over it.

Her brother Chris was on the floor. He was watching TV.

She stepped over him and went up the stairs.

Her cowgirl boots clicked hard.

In her bedroom she opened her cupboard door.

She climbed behind her clothes.

Yes. Everything was there.

She was ready to solve the crime.

Chapter 5

Dawn opened her eyes. It was Saturday morning.

She slid out of bed. She put on the new top Noni had made. She pulled on her jeans with the hearts.

She dragged the box out of the cupboard.

It was a wonderful box. It was big and white. It had fat pink polka dots.

Noni had bought it for her birthday.

Noni knew she wanted to solve mysteries.

She opened the box. Inside was everything she needed.

On top was a polka dot hat. It was pink, too. A blue eye was painted on the front.

She pushed it down on her head.

It was much too big. She couldn't see.

She stuck some paper inside.

In the mirror she looked great. No one would know about the paper.

She went down for breakfast.

Chris was watching TV. He had a bowl of cornflakes on the rug.

He was leaning over it.

Drops of milk were all over the rug.

"Daddy's going to kill you," Dawn told him.

"Get lost, pinhead," he said. He took a huge spoonful of cereal.

Then he looked at her.

He started to laugh.

Cornflakes flew all over the place.

"That hat," he said. He slapped his leg.

Dawn stepped over him. "It's my detective hat."

"It must be a size one hundred," he said.

She went into the kitchen.

Her father was standing at the sink. He was eating an orange.

"Where's Mummy?" Dawn asked.

"She's still asleep," he said. "She worked hard all week. Noni, too."

"How do you like my hat?" Dawn asked. She pushed it up.

Her father looked as if he were going to laugh. "It's fine," he said. "I see it has a private eye on the front."

Dawn nodded. "I don't know why."

"People call detectives private eyes," he said.

"Do they?"

"Detectives watch," said her father.

"They see things. Then they can solve crimes."

He tossed her an orange.

She missed.

It rolled on the floor.

"Sorry," her father said.

"It's all right." She picked up the orange. "I'm not a great catcher." She peeled it. She popped a piece into her mouth.

Her father poured her a bowl of cornflakes. "You're a great detective."

"Right." She started to eat as fast as she could.

"Slow down," her father said.

She chewed a little slower.

"I wanted to be a detective," her father said. He looked up at the ceiling. "I was seven years old."

"Why didn't you?"

42

He laughed. "I never could find a crime to solve."

Dawn looked at her cereal.

She wanted to tell about the ring.

She picked up her spoon.

She couldn't, though. Then she'd have to tell about the unicorn.

Her father would find out she had taken it.

He'd feel sad.

She'd better not tell him.

She ate the last cornflakes.

"I'm going out," she said.

"Me, too," said her father. "I think I'll rake the garden."

"I'm going to take my detective box," she said. "It has lots of good stuff."

"I hope you find a crime to solve," he said.

Dawn went back to her bedroom for the box.

It was heavy.

She lugged it downstairs.

Chris started to laugh again.

"Bean nose," she told him.

She went out of the door.

She'd go to school.

She'd look all over the place.

She'd solve the crime—one, two, three.

Dawn the detective.

Dawn the private eye.

She went down the street.

It was a good thing it was Saturday. She didn't want to see anybody.

They'd stare at her. They'd say she had taken the ring.

She put the detective box down.

It was heavy.

She blew on her fingers. She pushed her hat out of her eyes.

Then she saw somebody.

Jason Bazyk.

At least, it looked like Jason. Same brown hair. Same ears.

He bumped into a tree.

Yes. That was Jason.

He was carrying a brown paper bag.

Dawn grabbed her box. She ducked behind Mrs Moley's tree.

She tried to make herself skinny and small.

She'd have to wait until Jason went away.

She hoped he'd hurry up.

Chapter 6

Dawn peeped out at Jason.

He was looking all around.

He hid behind a letterbox.

Then he ran to Mrs Nelson's tree.

Dawn took a deep breath. She ran behind the stop sign. She peeped again.

What was Jason doing?

He must be crazy.

He dashed across the street and went through the school gate.

Too bad. She'd have to sit here and wait.

That could be all day.

Snaggle doodles. That's what Emily Arrow always said.

Double snaggle doodles.

Dawn sat down on a pile of leaves.

She opened her box.

She threw some of the stuff on the ground. She looked until she found what she wanted.

A pair of fake glasses.

She put them on.

Then she pushed her hair up under her hat.

What next?

She could put on the fake furry brown moustache.

No good.

Jason would know a kid wouldn't have a moustache.

Too bad she wasn't tall.

She tore the moustache in two pieces.

She stuck them on her eyebrows.

She looked in the mirror inside the box.

Great.

She looked like an ugly old man.

A very little ugly old man.

She put everything back in the box. She went into the school playground.

She took little hopping steps. Jason would never know who she was.

Jason didn't even see her.

He walked around to the front door. He tripped up the step.

Dawn watched him.

He dusted off his jeans.

He tried to open the door.

It was locked.

Dawn ducked behind the swings.

Jason tried the back door next.

It pulled open.

He looked around. Then he rushed inside.

Dawn sat down on the swing to think.

She gave herself a little push.

Why was Jason sneaking around?

Why was he going to school on a Saturday?

And why was he carrying a brown paper bag in his hand?

Maybe he had taken Emily's ring.

Maybe he was going to take something else.

She had to find out.

She hopped over to the back door.

It took a long time, but Jason might be looking out of the window.

Slowly Dawn opened the door.

No one was in the hall.

She listened. She couldn't even hear Jason's footsteps.

She tiptoed down the corridor.

It was hard to be quiet with her boots on.

Next time she'd wear her plastic sandals.

She sat on the floor and pulled one boot off.

Then she pulled off the other one.

Where could she hide them?

If Jim the caretaker came along, he'd throw them away.

Jim liked a clean school.

She'd have to go upstairs. She'd put them in the classroom.

She started to stand up.

Then she heard a noise.

A slithering noise.

A whooshing sound.

Something dropped over her head.

She couldn't see. She couldn't breathe.

She opened her mouth wide.

She couldn't even scream.

Chapter 7

"Gotcha!" someone yelled.

Dawn reached up. She pulled at the thing on her head.

It was ripping.

Crackling.

What was it?

"Thief!" the voice yelled.

"Help!" Dawn screamed.

She tore at the thing.

It came off in her hand.

A paper bag. Jason's paper bag.

And there was Jason. "Thief!" he yelled again.

Then his mouth opened. He looked at her. "Dawn Bosco?"

Dawn took off her glasses. She put

them in her pocket. Then she began to pull on her boots. "I'm getting out of here," she said. "You're crazy, Jason Bazyk."

"Dawn Bosco," he said again.

"You were trying to kill me."

"Dawn Bosco," he said for the third time.

Dawn pulled on her other boot. "Don't keep saying that."

"I thought someone was following me," he said in a loud voice. "A little old man in a huge polka dot hat. With glasses. With eyebrows."

Dawn put her hand up to her face.

"Only one eyebrow now," Jason said. "It's stuck on your forehead."

He sat down on the floor. "Whew. I'm glad it's you."

"What are you doing here?" she asked. "Sneaking around."

"I'm going to be a detective when I grow up."

"Hey," said Dawn. "Me too. Or a school crossing guard."

"I'm trying to find something out," Jason said. He stood up. "Who took Emily Arrow's ring?"

"That's why I'm here," said Dawn. "It wasn't me."

"I didn't think so," said Jason. "Let's go."

"I'm ready. Where?"

Jason shook his head. "I don't know."

"To the art room cupboard. Of course. That's where it started."

"Wait a minute," Jason said. He turned his head. "Did you hear a noise?"

"Lots of noise," Dawn said. "You

talk noisily. You walk noisily, too."

"That's what my mother says," Jason said. "I hear another noise, too."

"It's Jim," said Dawn. "He's cleaning."

"Maybe we shouldn't be here." Jason looked worried.

"Jim won't mind. We can ask him about the ring. Maybe he found it last night."

They went down the corridor.

Dawn stopped to look out of the window. "I think it's going to rain."

"I'm supposed to be at home when it rains," said Jason.

"Don't worry. We have time," Dawn said. She took a breath. "Uh-oh."

"What's the matter?"

"Do you still hear that noise?"

"You mean Jim?" asked Jason. "Of

course I do."

Dawn pointed. "Jim's outside. He's raking up leaves."

Jason looked down the corridor. "Someone's there," he said.

"Maybe a teacher," Dawn said. "Maybe someone forgot their home-work."

"We could go home," Jason said. "It's going to rain anyway."

"Let's see who it is," Dawn said. She started down the corridor. "We'll take a peep."

She looked at her boots again. "I have to take them off," she whispered. "They make too much noise."

She slipped them off quickly.

She left them in the corridor.

"I think someone's in the music room," Jason said.

"Or the art room," said Dawn.

Jason went to the music room. He banged open the door.

"Shh," Dawn said. "The whole world can hear you."

She went to the art room.

The door was open.

She put her head around it.

Someone was standing next to the window.

It was Jill Simon. She was holding Beast's clay string bean.

"Hey!" Dawn said.

Jill was wearing a ring. A gold ring. It had a blue stone.

"Hey," Dawn yelled again.

Jill's mouth opened. She started to screech.

She ran past Dawn. She raced out of the door.

Halfway down the corridor, she took a huge hop.

She sailed over Dawn's boots.

A moment later she was gone.

Jason came out of the music room. "Who was screaming?" he asked. He fell over Dawn's boots. "Wasn't that Jill Simon?" He rubbed his knee.

"Wearing Emily Arrow's ring," said Dawn.

"Jill Simon?" Jason said.

"A thief," said Dawn.

"Jill Simon," Jason said again. "I can't believe it."

"Stop saying that," Dawn said. "Let's go. We have to catch her."

Chapter 8

Outside it was pouring with rain.

Big drops bounced off the pavement.

Dawn and Jason stood at the open door.

Jill was nowhere in sight.

"I think I'd better go home," Jason said.

"Not me," said Dawn. "Carmen stays out in the rain. Policemen stay out in the rain. The postman walks around in the rain, too."

"You're right," said Jason.

He ran back down the corridor.

He grabbed the torn paper bag. "I'll stick this over my head."

"And I've got my hat," said Dawn.

She pushed it out of her eyes.

They ran out of the playground. They crossed the street and turned the corner.

"There she is," Dawn said.

"Stop thief!" Jason yelled.

Jill didn't look back. She hopped over a puddle.

"Faster!" yelled Dawn.

"My paper bag is wet!" Jason yelled. He pulled it off his head.

Dawn reached up.

Her hat was gone.

"Wait." She looked back. A fat polka dot hat was floating in a puddle.

"Don't stop," Jason called. He splashed through the puddles.

Dawn took a breath. She kept going.

They caught up with Jill on Linden Avenue.

Dawn reached out for her arm.

Jill spun around. "Dawn Bosco," she said. "Jason Bazyk."

"Who did you think?" Jason asked. "Santa Claus?" He began to laugh.

"Watch out," Jill said. "I just saw a—" She stopped. She raised her shoulder. "A horrible boy. He had a moustache growing out of his forehead."

Jason couldn't stop laughing. He kept pointing to Dawn.

"That was me," said Dawn. "Just me."

She took Jill's hand. She pointed to the ring.

"Where did you get this?" she asked. "On the art room sink?"

"No," Jill said. "At Lacy's department store."

Dawn shook her head. "Listen, Jill. This is Emily Arrow's ring."

"She's right," Jason said. "Same gold ring. Same blue stone."

"No." Jill began to shake her head.

At the same time Dawn opened her mouth. "Wait a minute."

"I can't wait," Jill said. "It's pouring down."

"Something's wrong," Dawn said.

"Yes," said Jason. "It's wrong to take a ring. It's wrong to say you got it at Lacy's."

Dawn stood up straight. "Sorry, Jason. Jill's not the thief."

"Of course she is," said Jason. "Same gold ring. Same blue—"

"Stop saying that," Dawn said. "Look at the ring."

"Same blue—" Jason began. He opened his eyes. "No crack."

"That's right," Dawn said. "Emily's

ring had a crack in it."

"Of course Emily's ring had a crack," Jill said. "She banged it on the swings."

Rain dripped off Jill's chin. "Goodbye," she said. "I'm going home. I'm going to watch TV."

She started to run.

"Hey!" Dawn called. "Why were you at school?"

Jill turned around. She looked as if she were going to cry. "I hate my onion. I was going to make something else. A string bean, maybe."

"Beast made the string bean," Dawn said.

"I know," said Jill. "I was looking at it. I was looking at Emily's carrot, too. I couldn't think of another vegetable to make."

Jill wiped away another drop of rain. She began to run.

Jason shook the water out of his shoes. "See you," he said to Dawn.

He started to run, too.

Dawn walked back for her hat.

It was silly to run, she thought.

She was soaking wet anyway.

Chapter 9

Dawn was standing in the art room.

An onion jumped off the windowsill.

So did a string bean.

Emily Arrow's cucumber rolled up to her. "Thief!" it yelled.

"Lumpy old cucumber!" Dawn shouted. "You can't even roll right."

"Time to get up," her mother said.

She opened her eyes. It was Monday. School.

She still hadn't solved the mystery.

She sat on the side of her bed. She didn't want to get dressed.

"Hurry up, Toots," her mother called.

She looked at her cowgirl boots. They were still wet.

So was her polka dot hat.

She slid into her green plastic sandals.

She reached into her detective box and pulled out a badge.

It said: POLKA DOT PRIVATE EYE

It looked great on her pink shirt.

In the kitchen she ate her cornflakes.

She didn't talk.

She had to think hard.

Somehow she had to find out about Emily's ring.

She talked to herself on the way to school.

"The art room sink," she said. "All of us were there."

She counted on her fingers. "Me. Linda. Jill. And Emily."

Everyone had been laughing.

Well, not everyone.

She and Emily had been pushing a little.

She remembered the ring on the sink.

The soapy ring.

She stopped in the playground.

Wait a minute, she told herself. That ring wasn't Emily's. It was Jill's.

Emily was sitting on a swing.

Dawn went up to her. "I have bad news. Your ring wasn't in the art room. I never saw it."

"I had it in art," Emily said. She gave a push with her foot. She sailed up in the air. "I wish someone would believe me."

"I believe you."

Emily raised her arms on the swing chains. She stood up on the swing.

"You're not supposed to stand up," Dawn said. "Don't get into trouble."

"I won't," said Emily. She smiled at Dawn.

"I didn't take your ring," Dawn said.

"I believe you," said Emily.

Just then the bell rang.

They ran for the big brown doors.

In the classroom, Dawn took out her notebook.

They had to copy a story.

The story was about salad.

Not vegetables again! Dawn thought.

Jason looked back at her. He made a face, too.

She started to copy what Ms Rooney had written.

Eat a salad every day.

Slice up some tomatoes.

Add some cucumber.

Put them on lettuce.

Salad is good for you.

Dawn looked up. Something was bothering her.

What was it?

She closed her eyes.

She took a breath. Salad. Vegetables.

Her eyes flew open. "Snaggle doodles," she shouted. "I just thought of something."

Jason turned around. He made crazy eyes at her.

"I know where Emily Arrow's ring is," she said.

Chapter 10

Everyone stopped writing.

Emily Arrow put down her pencil.

Ms Rooney stood up from her desk.

"I know where your ring is," Dawn told Emily again.

"Where?" Emily asked.

"Where?" asked Jason.

"Yes," said Ms Rooney. "For goodness' sake! Tell us where."

Dawn went to the front of the room.

She stood on tiptoes.

Ms Rooney bent down.

Dawn whispered in Ms Rooney's ear.

Ms Rooney smiled. "I bet you're right."

Ms Rooney clapped her hands. "Line

up, class. Let's go and see if Dawn Bosco can find Emily's ring."

Dawn rushed to the front of the line.

Emily Arrow rushed to the front of the line, too.

Then she stepped back. "You go first," she told Dawn.

"No, you," said Dawn.

Jill Simon stepped in front of them. "I'll go first," she said.

They started down the corridor.

"Hey!" Jill turned round. "I don't even know where we're going."

"To the art room," said Dawn.

"Right," said Ms Rooney.

They passed the headmaster's office. Mr Mason was coming out of the door.

"We're on our way to solve a mystery," said Ms Rooney. "Dawn Bosco is our class detective."

Mr Mason winked at Dawn. "It's always good to have a private eye around," he said.

They turned the corner and stopped at the art room door.

Mrs Kara was there. She was putting pieces of green wool on everyone's desk.

She straightened up. "Today the sixth year are going to make tablecloths," she told Ms Rooney.

Dawn wished she were in the sixth year.

She'd love to make a tablecloth.

They marched into the art room.

"Wait a minute," said Mrs Kara. "You're not the sixth year."

Everyone laughed.

Ms Rooney put her arm around Dawn's shoulders. "Dawn has something to show us," she said.

Dawn walked over to the windowsill. Outside she could see Carmen, the crossing guard. She was blowing her whistle.

Dawn walked along next to the sill. She looked at the vegetables.

They were hard now, not so grey any more. They looked white.

She picked up Emily Arrow's cucumber.

It was a terrible cucumber.

One end was skinny.

The other end had a fat lump.

Dawn picked up the cucumber. "Sorry, Emily," she said.

She smashed it down on the sink.

Bits of hard clay flew up all over the place.

Inside was a ring.

A gold ring with a blue stone.

A cracked blue stone.

"I can't believe it," Emily said. She gasped. "I remember now. I took off my ring. I didn't want to get clay on it."

Everyone laughed.

"I must have rolled it into my cucumber," Emily said.

"Good work," Jason told Dawn.

"Excellent," said Ms Rooney.

"I thought it was a carrot," said Jill.

Dawn looked out of the window again.

Carmen looked up and saw her.

They waved at each other.

Dawn couldn't wait for school to be over.

She had to tell Carmen about the ring.

She'd ask Emily to come with her.

She and Emily would go home together.

She still had some clay—red, and yellow, and green.

They'd make some vegetables, or rings, or maybe a polka dot hat.